Robert Draper

Early Aspirations

A Private Collection of Poems

Robert Draper

Early Aspirations
A Private Collection of Poems

ISBN/EAN: 9783337182984

Printed in Europe, USA, Canada, Australia, Japan

Cover: Foto ©Andreas Hilbeck / pixelio.de

More available books at **www.hansebooks.com**

EARLY ASPIRATIONS:

A

PRIVATE COLLECTION OF

POEMS

By ROBERT DRAPER.

—

1883.

TO

My Children,

WITH THE FERVENT HOPE THAT THEIR LIVES MAY BE FILLED

WITH NOBLE AIMS, AND

THAT, UNDER A KIND PROVIDENCE, THEY MAY BE ABLE

TO DO MORE AND BETTER THAN THEIR

Father.

PREFACE.

This little collection of poems is made with a twofold purpose: one being to gather together the occasional thoughts, mainly of earlier years, to preserve for my own gratification: the other, that I may be enabled to present to my friends a private testimonial of esteem. It is to be hoped they may not prove an infliction instead of a pleasure.

They stand in the order in which they were written, and probably that is the best form in which to place such fugitive efforts; while, at the same time, it preserves, in a measure, the line of my own thought and experience.

Before receiving the printer's benediction, some wild branches have been pruned off, and some sprigs of later thought have been added. I am still conscious of their defects, but they are the best that I can offer from the limited time and opportunities I have been able to command. I may add that nothing would give me more sincere delight than to have found the way to enrich them by a higher culture, a larger knowledge, and a deeper reflection. But sharp experience has taught me that the duties and necessities of life build stern limitations, and that the hard and exhausting struggle for existence and advancement soon clips the wings of imagination and makes short work with poetical dreaming. But the little accomplished I now venture to send forth on private rambles, knowing that, from my friends, their shortcomings will be tenderly received, and whatever merit they may possess will be fully accorded.

R. D.

Canton, Mass., Feb. 16, 1883.

CONTENTS.

———

8 CONTENTS

EARLY ASPIRATIONS.

GIVE PRAISE TO GOD.

I.

Give praise to God! to Him be given
The praises of both earth and heaven :
Let their united voices raise
A mighty song of joy and praise.

II.

Praise Him who robes the earth with light.
And folds it in the shades of night ;
Who holds the seasons in his hand
To fill with blessings every land.

III.

Praise Him who built th' eternal hills,
The valleys who with verdure fills;
Whose power pervades the mighty deep,
Whose love and mercies never sleep.

IV.

Praise Him who arched the heavens on high,
And filled with stars the gleaming sky;
Praise Him who framed the human mind
In truth and goodness God to find.

V.

Praise Him, ye nations of the earth!
Praise Him who gave creation birth,
Praise Him who still the work prolongs,
Praise Him to whom all praise belongs!

1854.

AFLOAT.

Once more upon the living wave, where, boys, we love to be,—
The dome of heaven above our heads,—beneath, the rolling sea ;
The heaving bosom of the deep makes ours in concord throb,
Its grandeur grows into our souls, and brings us close to God!

Sweep on, ye glorious winds, sweep on ! ye gray old billows, roll !
The freedom of the deep alone can fill the sailor's soul !
Thank God that only one-fourth land the wide world's beauty mars,
While waters thrice as wide reflect the glory of the stars !

Where'er the bounding billows roll, our noble bark may ride,
The welcome winds shall bear us o'er the ever friendly tide ;
Enough that we may plough the main, no bounds to dim our bliss,
Save where the circumambient skies and ocean meet to kiss !

No sculptured stone shall mark the spot where we to earth return ;
The billows that in life we loved, in death, shall be our urn ;
The mighty deep alone should hold the ashes of the free,
And our requiem be chanted by the ever-sounding sea.

Roll on, thou ever-changing sea! in majesty sublime,
Lave with thy blessings every shore, and hallow every clime ;
In tenderness upon thy breast the mighty ages sleep,
And He, who guides eternal power and grandeur guards the deep!

1854.

THE SUNDAY SCHOOL.

I.

How BLEST is the hour when the children assemble,
And childhood and youth lift their spirits in song ;
Where the heart learns to love and to trust, not to tremble ;
Where, in love of the pure and the true, we grow strong.

II.

Surely this is God's garden, for here are the fairest
And loveliest flowers that can gladden the earth ;
For the flowers of the heart yield a fragrance the rarest
Where purity blossoms and faith has its birth.

III.

With offerings unstinted, with radiant delight,
Let heart, mind, and means for the children have play ;
Fill their young hearts with courage to live what is right.
To the sunlight of God point them ever the way.

1854.

THE DAY OF JUDGMENT.

[Matthew xxiv., 29-31.]

THICK darkness shall mantle the earth and the sky,
And the waters with frenzy shall rush from on high ;
The earth shall wax faint, and in wonder the skies
Shall stoop when Jehovah in judgment shall rise.

The sun shall become but a cold, dusky ball,
And the stars from their orbits in horror shall fall ;
Heaven's thunders shall roll like the clouds at his feet,
And her lightnings shall blaze through the farthest retreat.

So Jehovah shall come in his glory and might,
E'en the angels of God shall be awed at the sight ;
The curtains of heaven shall roll back as a scroll,
While the Universe groans and surrenders its soul.

Then his angels shall soar o'er the sea and the land,
And above the loud thunder the trumpet shall sound ;
And Earth shall her millions upheave at the blast,
And Ocean his burden to judgment shall cast.

Then the Judge of the world, in pavilions of light,
With swift justice the wrongs of all nations shall right,
And mete with just measure their honor or shame,
Nor a tear, nor a pang, unrequited remain !

And the glass which so darkly now hideth his ways
With his Fatherly Love shall triumphantly blaze ;
And Justice and Truth crowned with glory shall rise
As Time in the arms of Eternity dies.

1851.

POETICAL EPISTLE TO J. H.

CANTON, Feb. 1, 1855.

DEAR JOE, I gladly take my pen
To bear my love, and tell again
How fact and fancy circle round
This rocky, bleak, terrestrial ground.

Kind Providence her matchless wealth
Bestows in all-abounding health ;
Were all the world like our sweet plain,
Pandora could no longer reign.
The bracing air, so pure and good,
Works like a tonic in the blood ;
And health in every vein will dance
Where sense and nature have a chance.
And Esculapius, with his pills
And fostering care of petty ills,
May take a long and quick farewell,
And laughing Health with us will dwell.
No sleek M.D.'s we care to see,
Who sponge a fortune, called a fee ;
And well can spare the soulless hacks,
The nostrumed horde, the murdering quacks,
And half-taught, bogus-titled knaves,
Who learn their trade by filling graves.

The stream of trade is sluggish now
As water in a Western slough;
The hum, the snap, the charm, has fled,
And industry lies cold and dead.

    While work is slack and times are dull,
Hard at the 'rithmetic I pull,
With grammar or a little rhyme ;
But more than all I crowd the time
With delving into ancient tomes
Where empires bud and crumble thrones.
The mighty deeds, my thoughts engage,
On Rollin's panoramic page,
And Plutarch's heroes live again
To mould and fashion noble men.
For we were early taught, you know,
That active minds to triumph go ;
That busy hands have naught to fear,
And keep old Satan in the rear.

King Winter, grand and stern and wild,
With bannered hosts and artist guild,
Goes whistling through the frozen skies,
While o'er the world his mantle lies ;
And keenly through the leafless trees
Careers the hyperborean breeze.
The heavens are cold, the earth is dead,—
The soul of '54 has fled ;
And cold as charity, dear Joe,
Is piled around th' unblushing snow.

Though eighteen circling years have shed
Their lights and shadows o'er my head,

I have not yet secured a wife
To jog along with me through life ;
In gladness, all my joys to share,
And temper every breath of care ;
To cheer, to comfort, and to throw
A halo o'er my path below.
But, still, I hold it best to take
A hint from nature, and to mate
When manhood's vigor hails its spring,
While Hope is on her morning wing,
Ere one dull, sordid aim we form,
And pass the rose to pick the thorn.

    To meet the stern demands of life
I want no gewgaw for a wife ;
No glitter, frippery, or pretence
Must take the place of common sense ;
No saucy, independent air,
Her sex unsexing, must she wear ;
But strength with sweetness may she blend,
With noble aims may vigor wend,
And may the WOMAN, clear and strong,
Cleave fast to right, smite hard the wrong.
I seek a girl whose heart shall be
From pride and affectation free ;
Transparent truth her eyes must speak,
And nature only tinge her cheek ;
Refined in feeling, thought, and word,
And blithe and cheery as a bird ;
Whose modest, simple tastes disclose
The selfsame hand that paints the rose.

    A temper sweet I hope to find,
Health waiting on a well-stored mind :

Whose heart responds to mine, as true
As thirsty flowers to evening's dew;
Whose aim shall be to build her throne
Amid the calm delights of home,
And make that realm of priceless worth
The best-loved spot in all the earth,—
Where sweet content and peace shall kiss,
And mutual love make perfect bliss;
Where sickly shams and shows must stop,
And o'er that threshold enter not,
Nor hollow-eyed Appearance rise
To blur our comfort and our joys.

   A voice like music, soft and clear,
To soothe the soul and charm the ear,
A matchless form and classic face
The idol of my soul *may* grace;—
But fresh as ever wild-flower blew,
And pure as lily ever grew;
Whose principles as instincts flame
Where even thought could leave a stain;
Whose love will wear, and brightest glow
When trial clouds the way below;
And native goodness is the ray
That gilds with glory all her way:—
These are the life-charms, fond and fair,
Her radiant soul must ever wear;
These are the graces which control
The holiest memories of the soul.

Dear Joe, I now will say good-by,
  For this time and occasion;
And may your breast ne'er heave a sigh
  Nor know a lone sensation.

And may your eye be always glad,
And may your heart be never sad,
And when life's battles called to fight
Just stick like beeswax to the right.

    And, when upon old friends you call,
Please give my kind regards to all ;
And to your worthy self consigned
    Within this humble paper,
The best love and good wishes find
    Of your nephew,— ROBERT DRAPER.

BALANCES.

WHAT trials and troubles attend us each day,
    They track every footstep below ;
Anxiety harries each step of our way,
    And care lines the path as we go.

Scourged, racked, and borne down in the merciless strife,
    The crushed soul in rebellion may rise :
Does not Fate clamp to one the rough battle of life
    And toss to another the prize ?

Perchance we have thought that the burden is more
    Than the over-strung heart can sustain ;
Perchance, when the spirit is weary and sore,
    E'en the faith lodged above me may strain.

Are our spirits then made of such pitiful stock
    That troubles affright and dismay ?
Grim struggles the cradle of manhood must rock,
    And rend the soul's fetters of clay.

The allotments of Fate are but bald, mocking lies,
    The crown is for him who strives best :
The heart knows a great Providence rules in the skies,
    And His ord'rings are all for the best !

When by burdens bowed low, if our spirits will rise,
    Then His arm helps us over the way ;
When grief wrings the heart, if we look to the skies,
    The darkness will yield to the day.

The sorrows we carry in silence and tears,
    When sympathy mocks the torn breast,
Only God can assuage and give light to the years,
    Ere our loved ones again we may press.

It is something to *trust*, when the shadows of life
    Come down, and we scarce know the way :
Why lash, unavailing, the spirit to strife,
    With the promise of strength as our day ?

Can man fix a star on its throne in the sky,
    Or call forth a flower from the soil ?
Can he marshal the secrets that gird the Most High,
    Or add to the wisdom of God ?

Do the oaks of the forest attain the same height ?
    Neither all can endure the same strain ;
And a sweet voice within tells me all will be right,—
    Shall a mortal his Maker arraign ?

Around us the tempests of trial may crash,
    Nor fear our serenity shroud :
Through doubting and darkness, His lightnings will flash
    When the soul sweeps the blue o'er the cloud.

When the storm darkly gathers, give Duty the wheel ;
     Brave hearts round the sharp back of care ;
With high trust we advance as with sinews of steel,
     And smile o'er the crags of despair !

Far be it from me at my lot to repine ;
     And, where'er o'er the earth I may range,
May my aim be to render my living divine,
     Till He bids me my residence change.

1855.

ELIJAH'S SIGN TO DETERMINE THE TRUE GOD.

FULL three circling years over Israel's plains
 The fountains of heaven had been sealed in the skies,
Till the sore, blistered earth her sweet service disclaims,
 And Judæa in ashes and barrenness lies.

O Israel! how oft shall the lesson be told?
 That, when God is forgotten, calamity reigns ;
But, when righteousness rules,— still, the story of old,—
 By his bounties Jehovah his blessing proclaims.

To the gods that are false, the false Ahab is led,
 Round his ways are the meshes of Jezebel's wiles,
And Asherah's priests at her table are fed,
 And the prophets of Baal wax strong in her smiles.

Then Elijah, God's prophet, so simple, so grand,
 Bade the people to truth lay the plummet and line :
" Between halting opinions how long will ye stand ?
 If the Lord then be God, let us prove for all time."

Then the prophets of Baal and he of the Lord
 Assembled on Carmel to prove the true God,—
To reveal the Supreme, and whose will had deferred
 The rain, when gaunt famine was stalking abroad.

And this did Elijah convey as a sign :
   " Let him be your God that shall answer by fire ;
Choose a bullock, and raise it aloft on your shrine,
   And then call on your gods to enkindle the pyre."

Then the zealots of Baal brayed forth from the morn
   Until noon, but no token their strained vision meets ;
When Elijah exclaimed, with derision and scorn,
   " Cry aloud, he's a god, peradventure he sleeps ! "

Gashed and gory, again the dupes howled with their might,
   Still the altar was cold, and unanswered their cries : —
Confounded is man when he strays from the right,
   For his Baals are deaf unto all but his joys.

Then twelve stones took the prophet to Israel's name,
   And an altar he reared in the name of the Lord,
Where his offering he placed for the hallowing flame,
   And thrice o'er the shrine the prized water he poured.

Then Elijah, with fervor and zeal, said, " This day,
   Great God of our fathers, throughout Israel's land,
Show thou only art God ! "   Even as he did pray,
   The sign that he sought was advancing, at hand.

For down from the skies came the fire of the Lord,
   And a glowing incension the altar enwreathed ;
And the people bowed low, for their hearts were appalled :
   " The Lord, he is God ! " was the murmur they breathed.

Men may bow to their Baals of pleasure or power,
  Or the almighty Mammon their vision may blind;
But, if shadows they trust in prosperity's hour,
  When they look for a God, but a phantom they find.

Truth, exiled from earth, will descend from the sky,
  Though bigots may howl, and though tyrants assail;
And imposture's wide hells yet clean open shall lie,
  For Israel's God in the end will prevail.

                                              1855

LINES WRITTEN IN A SICK ROOM AT MIDNIGHT.

WHILST we our vigils through the long night keep,
And watch with tender care the sick man's couch,
Steal in thy silence down, oblivious sleep,
And sweet repose unto the sufferer vouch.
But yesternoon, he walked in manhood's pride,
With promise of long, lusty years to run ;
But life and death move ever side by side,—
Ere down heaven's western slope had rolled the sun,
His glorious prime a blasted wreck was cast ;
Gone was the rugged health,— life's source of joys,—
The best inheritance that man can grasp,
Though held, a spendthrift's bauble, till it flies.
The unbroken line, the mighty multitude
From age to age go hurrying, jostling on,
And only pause beneath some fateful cloud,
Nor measure life while shines a prosperous sun.

O human life !   O love, hope, grief, and pain !
A few short, feverish years, and all is o'er :
Hushed is the grave alike to praise or blame,—
No penitential tears can e'er restore
The bloom of opportunity again,
No wrong undo, nor snatch life's gold from dross,—

God's gate is here! the petty pomps of men
The threshold of two worlds can never cross.
Vain is the shaft reared to neglected worth,
No hot remorse can warm Death's icy hand;
But heaven's own bliss may nestle round the earth,
If well we overstep Time's drifting sand.

1855.

THE DEITY.

I.

FATHER of light! of light the sun,
   Immensity thy name surrounds :
Man's reason fails to grasp the sum,
   Which his poor feebleness confounds.

II.

When scenes stupendous greet the eye,
   Proportioned praise shall we divorce?
The spreading earth, the boundless sky,—
   Unoutlined grandeur guards their source.

III.

In God's great temple hushed we stand,
   And reverent awe the bosom thrills,
Though veiled is the Almighty hand
   That laid the deeps and reared the hills.

IV.

His presence fills the soul with awe
   Where oceans yawn or mountains climb ;
His wisdom girds the world with law,
   And leads the ancient steps of Time.

V.

He folds creation in his care,
  And binds it round with beams of light;
The day his matchless splendors bear,
  His glory heaven reveals by night.

VI.

His thought the frame of Nature cast;
  Her every nook his mercies fill;
His arm sustains the mighty Past;
  The Future hangs upon his will.

VII.

He guides the ages as they roll;
  He moulds the nations to his law;
And deep within the human soul
  Immortal hopes his love foresaw.

VIII.

His chariot is eternal Right,
  When clouds and darkness veil the skies;
And round about his throne of light
  Eternal truth and goodness rise.

IX.

In reverence we, his children, bend
  With childhood's sacred trust and love;
And may his smile our steps attend
  Through life, in death, and heaven above.

1855.

THE BLUES AND THE CURE.

For but sorrow alone should a mortal prepare ;
With the first beams of morn rolls the swift tide of care ;
And, as night from the skies drops her mantle of gloom,
His grim trooping woes bear him down to the tomb.

Pain, trouble, and grief,— grief, trouble, and pain,—
Is the chart of a day ; and all days are the same.
To fret, worry, and fume is the portion of man,
The fixed rut for the race, the unchangeable plan.

Anxiety blisters the sole and the palm,
And subsoils the heart as the yeoman his farm ;
On the smoothest of brows writes in wrinkles her frown,
And gnaws even the roots from the high-polished crown.

Care chases the saint, sinner, sage, and the fool,
Nor stagnation nor calm knows her well-paddled pool ;
And the way becomes darker the older we grow,
And each day that we live but increases our woe.

In misfortune we sour, and call friendship a lie :
But a truce to complaint,— let us fight till we die !
For a true independence no foe can e'er crush,
While the angel, Integrity, needs not to blush !

Meet misery's scowl with a conquering smile,
Hope nourishment lends, and grim care will beguile ;
Hands willing, heads clear, hearts sturdy and true,
Flash gleams through all clouds, and find stars peeping through !

Then, onward ! and be not a slave to despair,
Unstring not the will to heart-cankering care ;
Give your woes to the winds, and get hold of the right,
Then honestly, hopefully, manfully fight.

Drive on like the gale ; and, wherever you go,
With a hand for a friend, and contempt for a foe,
Trample obstacles down, or clean over them climb,
But keep sweetness and conscience, with grit, to the line.

1855.

EXTRACTS FROM A SACRED POEM ENTITLED "THE DESTRUCTION OF BABYLON."

ALMIGHTY GOD! Can man conceive in thought
Thy vast omnipotence? How vain to try!
He sees the worlds thy handiwork hath wrought,
Which all the rolling years of change defy;
Thine own handwriting overspreads the sky,—
Stars write the record of Almighty power;
Within thy hand, the mighty waters lie;
Thy presence dwells where mountain grandeurs tower:
All perfect nature's God, we find thee in each flower!

Father Divine! inspire my thought to trace
Thy righteous judgments, which are just and sure:
Thou art a God whence springs o'erwhelming grace,
Abundant mercy, patient to endure
The errant steps when worldly pleasures lure
Thy flocks astray; but, when triumphant waves
Sin's flaunting banner, then dost thou immure
Thy face in grief, while blushless Revel raves,
And foul Corruption fills the world with misery's waves?

From heaven's far ends he rolls Destruction's broods,
Earth-rocked convulsions at his bidding rise,
At his command the Deluge rolls her floods,
And tempests robed in flame invade the skies.
The God of armies, HE the battle guides!

The pride of Babylon must kiss the grave,
The doom of heaven on all her vileness lies ;
Fate's mystic words her palace walls invade :
When, madly, man fights God, he's but the Devil's slave.

Dash man's vain creeds and dogmas in the dust,
Make God in nature and his Word your guide ;
There build your fanes, let there repose your trust,
On his foundations bid the soul abide,
And firmest stand when most and sorest tried :
By Duty led, as Conscience dictates, DO !
Build deep, build broad, build strong, build high, build true :
Undying principles the long eternities sweep through.

                                                    1855.

PETITION OF THE HEART.

I.

Father of mercy, source of love!
　When all grows dark and hope seems gone,
When faint and weary, then, oh, give
　The faith to strive, and still press on.

II.

Help us to tread the narrow way
　Nor count the trial, pain, or loss;
To every night there comes a day,—
　A time to lay down every cross.

III.

Teach us how manhood must be won,
　How Christian fortitude is blest;
And, when our work on earth is done,
　Take us to Thine eternal rest.

1856.

SING YE TO THE LORD.

Sing ye to the Lord, lift the timbrels of gladness,
   The arm of Jehovah his people hath saved ;
He stayed the mailed hosts in their noonday of madness,
   And the dark waters rolled where their banners were waved.

At the prophet's grand mandate, swift back to their places
   Triumphantly surged the omnipotent waves :
They clasped the vast hosts in their fatal embraces,
   And the legions embattled went down to their graves.

Darkness hides the Almighty, but clear is his leading :
   To Freedom went Israel by fire and by cloud ;
And unteachable Egypt, to darkness receding,
   Sank as lead in the sea, with the sea for a shroud !

Pain chases the chariot by tyranny driven ;
   Every link is plague-festered which liberty chains ;
All the ages of bondage His vengeance hath riven,
   Forever the Lord God omnipotent reigns !

In glory triumphant he marshals the deep,
   And halts the proud nations defying his will ;
Not forever his wrath o'er injustice will sleep :
   Slow and sure down the ages Jehovah moves still !

1856.

TRUST.

I.

THE thunder hoarse may rend the skies,
  And devastation strew the plain,
In fear the trembling mountains rise,
  And chaos smite the roaring main.

II.

Though earth the elements should rend,
  And fierce commingling horrors pour,
Our God, our everlasting Friend,
  In season due will calm restore.

III.

Should danger's front our souls appall,
  His guardian care is o'er us still;
And yet, should even then we fall,
  We fall by His omniscient will!

IV.

Faith buoyed the ark which Noah bore
  When the dark waters veiled the land;
He sought, and found by him a shore
  Who holds the waters in his hand.

V.

So may we on life's ocean sail,
  Through days and weeks, through months and years,
Secure, though tempests should prevail,
  Till God, our Ararat, appears.

1856.

PRAYER FOR DIVINE GUIDANCE.

I.

Father Divine! thy love, thy light,
  Shed o'er our poor, uncertain way;
Through error guide our footsteps right,
  And lead us into truth's broad day.

II.

Shackle our faults to thy control,
  Bid passion's surging floods, "Be still";
Uproot each lust that rots the soul,
  And bend to thine the wayward will.

III.

While discord shakes on earth the breast,
  While fierce the fires of passion glow,
Far is thy bliss from such unrest,
  Oh, aid us heaven to find, below!

IV.

To gain the springs of human joy;
  Thy smile to win in every place;
To weigh not shadows as they fly;
  Thy goodness everywhere to trace.

V.

Lead us where it seems best to thee,
  With reason, faith, and love to cheer;
Then never from thee can we flee,
  And ever, Father, thou art near.

1856.

THE ONWARD COURSE OF TIME.

I.

On sternly sweeps despoiling Time,
    Worlds 'neath his awful steps decay ;
Man's proudest works, the vast, sublime,
    Oblivion darkly bears away.

II.

All eye can pierce, above, below,—
    In heaven's starred dome or earth we tread,—
Yet Time's effacing hand will throw
    O'er all, the mantle of the dead.

III.

Beneath the feet that empires crush —
    The hand that grasps Creation's soul —
Shall man with bold presumption rush,
    Whose life as fleeting day doth roll?

IV.

Youth opes with morning's blush life's page ;
    With mid-day's sun comes manhood's breath ;
Day's setting views his tottering age ;
    Night folds him in the arms of death.

V.

With every soul of human birth,
    Remorseless Time goes hurrying on ;
And soon the longest lines of earth
    In God's eternal cycles run.

1856.

MORNING.

Hail ! to the beams of opening day,
Silently bearing the night away ;
Hail to the light ! as the skies it fills
And breaks in beauty o'er the hills ;
Hail ! to the living, crimson glow,
Pouring joy o'er the world below :
The feet of Morn with glory shod
Seem to herald the march of God !

As the swift streamers of the dawn
Make proclamation of the morn,
The modest stars from view retire
Before th' advancing orb of fire.
And, as the glorious morning breaks,
The world to teeming life awakes ;
Earth's myriad forms of life begin
To lift their sacred morning hymn ;
Ten thousand feathered songsters raise
A mighty song of loving praise ;
Ten thousand forms of beauty glide
Unmarred by passion or by pride ;
And round the globe to greet the sun
With worship — only man is dumb.

1857.

WHAT MAN IS GREAT?

I.

WHAT man is great?   The man whose soul
Unyielding virtue doth control ;
Whose honor knows no shade of stain ;
Whose independence brooks no chain ;
Whose rectitude no art can warp ;
Whose conscience guides the helm of thought ;
Whose faith in God and truth and right
Is steadfast as the polar light ;
Who hates a wrong in every form,
And meets it with a giant scorn ;
Who frames his life by nature's rules,
Scorns social lies and Grundy fools,
Weak pride's disdain, bald self-conceit,
Loathes cunning's wiles and hates deceit ;
Whose instinct feeds on noble aims,
And low-born subterfuge disdains ;
Who makes simplicity his school,
Where pomp and ostentation rule ;
Whose life becomes a simple prayer
In God's great providential care.

II.

What man is great?   Can gold give birth
To deathless thoughts, to native worth ?
Will supple knees at Mammon's feet
Make hearts with pure affection beat ?

Shall bartered virtues honor bring,
Or social rank from knavery spring ?
Have claims alone the venal mart
Whose only home should be the heart ?
But he who kneels before a shrine
Above the power of chance or time
Has wealth that every ill defies,—
A spring of bliss that never dries.
And what is man, though he may tower
The slave of wealth, of fame, of power,
If love is cold, if honor sleeps,
If truth is dumb, if justice weeps ?
Mute be the harp of praise,— ay, brand
A fabric that can never stand ;
For what men by the devil gain
Sooner or later returns with shame.

III.

What man is great ?   The man whose soul,
When trial's storms around him roll,
Unshaken stands ; whose heart is stirred
To courage new from hopes deferred ;
Whose growing burdens prove a goad
To scale the sharp and thorny road ;
Who never faints, retreats, or whines,
But still the mount of triumph climbs ;
Who never stops to cosset care,
But meets it with an inward prayer ;
Though worn with toil, with grief, or woe,
Though misery's bitter cup o'erflow,
Though tempests of misfortune shed
Their withering blasts upon his head,—

Who scorns to yield whate'er oppose
While Duty bids him bear,— who throws
Defiance on the darkest fate
And nobly struggles on,— is great !
Who, though defeat each effort quell,
Knows " he who does his best does well " ;
Who, when life's conflicts fiercely fall,
By steeled endurance conquers all.

IV.

What man is great ?   'Tis he who stands
With generous breast and willing hands
To cheer and help at mercy's call,
To raise his fellows when they fall ;
To ease their agonizing throes ;
To stem the blasts of others' woes ;
To aid, where stern privations rest ;
To soothe, where anguish stabs the breast ;
Hearts bowed with wrongs to raise and cheer,
By deeds to dry the burning tear :
For man's true mission is to live
Each other happiness to give.
What bounds that mission shall be shown ?
Why bound the light from God's own throne ?
Where suns may rise, whilst ages roll
Its lines embrace the mighty whole.
And hath not Heaven the chiefest place
For those who best may serve their race ?

V.

What man is great ?   'Tis he whose light,
Whose only aim and guide, is Right !
And fire by night and cloud by day
Illumes and marks her royal way.

For Right strain every mortal nerve,
From that foundation never swerve ;
Press in her van, wherever thrust,
And in the "God of Battles" trust.
Will stricken Right e'er burst her tomb ?
Will rise the sun which sets in gloom ?
So prostrate Right in every form
Shall hail her resurrection morn ;
Sooner or later, from the skies,
The living mandate comes, Arise !
And man still learns in sorrow's school,
The Almighty lives, and Right must rule.

VI.

What man is great ?   Who builds the best
For life's great strife, for heaven's great rest ?
They are not always nearest God
Whose lives with great achievements throb ;
The noblest living is not found
In blazoned deeds or laurelled ground :
The grandest heroism ever shown
Perchance to God is only known.
He best fulfils his Maker's plan
Who proves in every place a MAN :
Whose courage breasts the rolling years,
And never flinches, tires, or fears ;
Whose love bears lightly every cross
Of circumstance, nor counts the loss ;
Who thrusts behind whate'er defiles,
And scorns temptation's liveried wiles ;
Who tramples down the devil Fraud,
By bribes unbought, by threats unawed ;

Who curries not to mortal man,
Loves honest worth, and hates a sham ;
Who rears himself a wrong to smite,
And lowly stoops to lift the right ;
Whose holy wrath injustice stirs,
Yet oft through soft-eyed mercy errs ;
Whose loving memory, green and sweet,
Each kindly act received will keep,
Yet who would tenfold favor do,—
Forget, and then the deed renew ;
Whose soul the praise of man may shun,
But listens low for Heaven's " Well done!"
These are the great ! for greatness sits
Upon his brow who well acquits
Himself of his God-given trust,
And proves kind, honest, faithful, just ;
Whose mind no superstitions sway,
But keenly watches every ray
That mellows, lifts, improves, expands,
That feeds the heart or nerves the hands
For noble effort, thought, or deed,
Unawed by priestly craft or greed,
By puling doubts or slavish fears,
Whose rectitude life's problem clears ;
Whose breast with sacred aims is strong,
And fears in thought to harbor wrong ;
Whose soul, when life's dark surges rise,
Takes chart and compass by the skies ;
Whose feet right's simple way have trod,
Then trusts, and leaves the rest with God.

1857.

LINES ON THE DEATH OF MISS M. C.

God's messenger came in the stillness of night
A welcome to bring from the regions of light,
And the blissful release in the smile we could trace
That the finger of Death had engraved on her face;
And she rose with no doubting, no tear, and no groan,
From the footstool of Time to Eternity's throne.
Though our life's blood is chilled as our loved ones depart,
Though the lone, narrow dwelling may pall the sad heart,
Still our hopes are undimmed, and Faith gilds every tear,
For the Mary we honored and loved is not here;
And enduring and steadfast remaineth our trust,
Though her perishing vestments are laid in the dust,
Through the ages to sleep 'neath the storm-beaten sod,
That her spirit went up to the home of its God.

1855.

LINES

WRITTEN UPON THE COMPLETION OF THE ATLANTIC CABLE.

God be praised! it is finished! All doubting is o'er,
  And astonishment thrills the long sea-severed lands.
Thought, flashed by the lightnings from shore unto shore,
  Makes a path through the deep, and the Nations shake hands!

For what is the waste of the wide-reaching sea
  When coursed by the Almighty's couriers of flame,
That await but the bidding of man ere they flee,
  His will to declare and his words to proclaim!

Their line has gone forth as a girdle of light,
  By fair Science led and all-conquering will ;
Their words to the ends of the world take their flight,
  Bearing glory to God, to man peace and good-will.

And hastening the dawn when the tribes of the earth
  Shall be joined as one family, kindred, and blood,—
This day has a nobler humanity birth,
  Prophetic with promise that reaches to God!

May the bonds which the mother and child now unite,
   While the rock-riven waves of old Ocean may roll,
Remain, and connect with omnipotent might
   Nations, Nature made kindred in thought and in soul.

May peace and good-will guard the path through the sea,
   Till, beyond resurrection, War moulds in his grave ;
With multiplied blessings may messages flee,
   And flash for proud Freedom till earth knows no slave.

1858.

FEBRUARY TWENTY-SECOND, 1859.

WHAT means yon distant booming gun,
    Resounding far o'er land and sea,
As years their annual courses run
    Throughout the Empire of the Free?
This day, what star arose to guide
    The struggling sons of Freedom on?
The star that set with glory dyed,
    The star the world calls Washington!

Who kneeled alone to Right and God,
    With firm and steadfast Truth allied;
Who in the path of Justice trod,
    And made Humanity his guide!
The good of every clime shall prize
    The honors he so nobly won;
And unborn millions yet shall rise
    To bless the name of Washington.

Shall we not, as yon cannon roars,
    Our grateful meed of praise impart
To him who sought these troubled shores
    To succor Freedom's found'ring ark?
Who fled from fortune, friends, and fame,
    From all a generous heaven decreed,
To Freedom's struggling sons, and came
    With them to battle and to bleed!

No rank or station proud could e'er
  Our venerated love control :
We view, through fame's and fortune's glare,
  His true nobility of soul.
Fixed is his star in Fame's proud skies,
  Which light to every age shall give :
Till Glory sleeps, till Freedom dies,
  The name of Lafayette shall live!

But words are weak for nature's kings,
  Whose hearts keep time to human needs ;
Who walk where Fate her shadow flings,
  And crown their lives with sacred deeds.
They are the sign-boards Heaven has set
  That we life's royal way may trace,—
These are the monarchs to whom yet
  Earth's sceptred dummies must give place!

And yet Columbia, even now,
  The favored child of Freedom stands,
The stain of slavery on her brow,
  The gore of bondage on her hands!
Blush, while that bitter speech is true,
  Which burns so long as lives the shame :
" I sorrow that my sword I drew
  To fasten on the negro's chain !"

Fair land! in more than name be free,
  Let Human Rights be deemed divine,
Let Freedom breathe from sea to sea,
  Let not complexion be a crime!

Not for ourselves alone should be
  The skies of Freedom ever blue :
Shine on, ye stars of Liberty,
  To *all* God's children always true !

The sacred instincts of our breast
  No Union of Crime shall own,
No hell-leagued Constitution wrest
  Heaven-whispering Conscience from her throne.
Our granite purpose will not yield
  While foul injustice blots thy sun ;
Though with our blood our vows are sealed,
  The negro's rights shall yet be won !

Peal on, thou thunder-throated gun,
  This day your loudest honors roll,
As years their annual courses run,
  And Freedom shout to every soul.
With heaven-fed faith, our march is — On !
  Till, under God, from sea to sea,
We make the land of Washington
  A *real* EMPIRE of the FREE !

STERLING TREASURES.

On, why do we prattle of riches and beauty!
  Will glorified puppets life's sunshine impart?
Heaven hears but the anthem of well-performed duty,
  And records but the deeds that give joy to the heart.

Beauty, I know, bears a passport to favor ;
  But, with naught to sustain it, how short is its reign !
And, if wealth does not blend with unselfish behavior,
  Its honors are libels and live but in name.

An affluent mind is the greatest of treasure ;
  A sweet disposition is beauty supreme :
The first will bequeath the serenest of pleasure,
  The last in the winter of age will be green.

They are friends no reverses of fortune can sway ;
  The darker our night, the more lustrous they shine ;
With unborrowed glory they gladden our way,
  And render the humblest of living divine.

They honor life's springtime, they hallow gray age ;
  On joy's solid foundation they help us to stand ;
And a far purer homage they ever engage
  Than mere beauty or riches can ever command.

1859.

GREAT JUDGE OF RIGHT.

GREAT Judge of Right, how long shall man
    On man his burning avarice urge?
How long shall he refuse to stem
    The hell of slavery's lava surge?
How long o'er Right shall triumph Wrong,
And Justice bend before the strong?

Behold the slave! Before heaven's sight
    Did clouds from woe and misery rise,
Then yon refulgent orb of light
    Would roll in darkness through the skies.
Will ne'er relentless man forego
To roll the tide of human woe?

How long shall men in bondage groan
    In lands where freedom mounts the skies?
How long shall man God's image own,
    To lash, to chain, and goad to sighs?
Ye Christian climes which freedom laves,
How long will ye give birth to slaves?

Your Christian boon is misery's sting,
    Nor bitterer Hell could ever plan:
For greed, man's Christian heart will wring
    Damnation on his fellow-man!
Should man too long scorn human laws,
Will Heaven not vindicate their cause?

To Heaven was borne the Hebrew's woes :
   Heaven heard : the Assyrian kissed the grave.
From Egypt's pride their cries arose:
   Heaven frowned : 'twas whelmed beneath the wave.
Injustice still to heaven doth groan,—
Man is the cause, and man alone !

Self centres in his little soul ;
   Expedience is his blighting creed ;
And Dura's god his endless goal,
   Though millions groan and millions bleed.
And this, where Christian temples rise
And point their fingers to the skies.

Gaze on the heavens, go scan the earth,—
   What doth the great "I AM " enthrall?
Free rose creation from its birth,
   And Freedom still encircles all.
Free is the light which heaven unbars
From God's great firmament of stars !

On every head the seasons smile,
   The waters brook not man's control,
The choiring wind is Freedom's child ;
   Unfettered. on the ages roll.
On all created good we see
God writes his own insignia,— FREE !

Yes, all is free ! Shall man alone,
   But little less than angels made,—
Shall man in hopeless bondage groan,
   And kneel before his God a *slave ?*
Where is the life of Calvary's creed?
In vain, in vain did Jesus bleed?

While mortals mar, high over all
　　God sees his children's heart-strings riven ;
Not e'en an honest tear can fall
　　But anguish dims the eye of Heaven.
Earth's needless tears and needless sighs
With grief would mantle all the skies !

To God, thy woes, Columbia, cry ;
　　To God goes up the slave's appeal :
God hears the wail of agony
　　Where'er his humblest children kneel.
God lives, God rules, Right knows no grave :
God will keep justice for the slave !

　　　　　　　　　　　　　　　　1859.

GOD OUR ETERNAL SUPPORT.

I.

BENEATH the silent tread of Time,
  Ages and empires pass away ;
The stars above us cease to shine,
  And oceans waste and skies decay.

II.

The mountains crumble into dust,
  The age-worn rocks to atoms fall ;
Still, man has for his steadfast trust,—
  Jehovah ruleth over all !

III.

Though Change the face of nature ploughs,
  Though Time the blossoms of the grave
Is wreathing upon human brows,
  One arm is still outstretched to save.

IV.

Though oceans waste and stars grow dim,
  Though all we love must pass away,
In perfect faith we look to Him :
  Th' unchanging God is still our stay !

1859.

FRAILTY OF HUMAN JUDGMENT.

WITH vision false and erring sense,
   We often blame and often praise,
Forgetting that Omnipotence
   The *motive* in the balance weighs.

The springs of action lie so deep,
   The pulse of self so strongly throbs,
The maze of garbs worn by deceit
   No eye may justly trace but God's.

Shall our imperfect judgment show
   The varying shades of good and ill?
Can we the silent forces know
   Which mould the heart and shape the will?

The beamless eye the mote may see,
   The faultless hand may cast the stone:
Till then, our brother's sins may be,
   Perchance, reflections of our own.

Not always what we deem a stain
   In God's pure light a stain will be;
And much we praise will reek with shame,
   Unveiled before eternity.

1859.

LINES SUPPOSED TO BE WRITTEN BY AN AMERICAN SLAVE.

O LAND of my fathers!   O land of my birth!
That spot, to my heart, o'er the wide-spreading earth,
Is the dearest, the loveliest,— even divine
Seems the home of my childhood, my own native clime.

Though a stranger, an exile, an alien, a slave,
Though in grief my gray hairs must go down to the grave,
Till memory shall shrink in oblivion's gloam
I will cherish the love of my African home!

Though o'er her in madness the harmattan sweeps,
Though the monsters of ocean may lout in her deeps,
Though death rides the sands of Sahara's vast sea,
Might I tread them again, where, at least, I was free!

Deem ye there that no oasis rises to cheer?
No zephyrs of gladness to dry sorrow's tear?
No swift-glancing waters of love and delight?
No glory-dyed noon and no grandeur-crowned night?

Whatever the shadows that over thee fall,
My country, I love thee! light, shadows, and all!
Would to God that my bones on thy hills had a grave,—
Accursed be the soil that I tread as a *slave!*

As I dwell on the themes that affection endears,
The rainbow of joy beams anew through my tears;
For joy's cup in my own heathen breast would o'erflow,
Ere the Christian (for Christ!) had baptized me with woe.

Though seared is my heart, still its wild throbs reveal
The depth of the fountains the breast may unseal:
How soul yearns to soul when love's tendrils find root!
Spring yielded its blossoms, but where is the fruit?

The wife of my bosom was dragged from my gaze,
And my chained hands to God but in prayer I could raise!
And the children she bore me, ay! where are they now?
For aye must the slave in Gethsemane bow?

As the lightning-rent oak of its foliage shorn,
As the mountain-bared rock rears its front to the storm,
So my heart is thus leafless and joyless and dead,
And, unsheltered, life's tempests sweep over my head.

Yet why for myself in bleared bitterness sigh,
While my countrymen groan 'neath the same brazen sky?
Shall one heart alone its black agony tell,
When four millions are writhing within the same hell?

From our tyrants no vestige of right can we claim;
On our virgins, they fasten pollution and shame;
And our manhood they crush and with infamy brand,
Lest the germ from Jehovah — the mind — should expand.

The life-freighted love of the mother, who spares?
Who pities her sorrows? who heedeth her prayers?
Who tempers the anguish that withers and brands
Her soul, when her child on the auction block stands?

Can a Being of Justice, of Mercy, and Love,
Gaze unmoved on these sky-piercing woes, from above?
Are no thunders of vengeance reserved where he dwells,
For these soul-blasting curses, these earth-rooted hells?

And, if so, may our wails of despair sweep on high,
And rain down on this land all the wrath of the sky!
And low, where the blackest of bondage doth frown,
May the scowl of the Almighty God settle down!

1859.

ADAM, OR THE FIRST MAN.

God looked upon the new-made earth,
And all that therein had their birth :
On night and day, on sea and sky
He gazed ; and, as beneath his eye
Unveiled the fair creation stood,
" He saw that everything was good."
But when his noblest work he viewed,
And traced the heart's cold solitude,—
Its pleading want, its aching ill
That Eden's garden could not fill,—
He saw, to crown creation's plan,
That there was wanting unto man
A kindred soul to fill his breast
With sweetness, harmony, and rest ;
With him to fall, with him to rise,
To share his sorrows and his joys ;
Whose harp with his should e'er attune
At morn, at eve, at night, at noon :
Nor yet the same,— a higher thought
Than yet the Hand Divine had wrought,
A purer and a holier flame
To halo round sweet woman's name !
A finer mould her form shall trace,
Transmuted with the soul of grace ;
With instincts as an angel's glance,
Her radiant thought shall thought entrance ;
Her breast with clinging love shall glow,
To star the brow of human woe ;

And lovely as an angel's dream
Shall woman on man's spirit gleam.
While less of earth, but more of sky,
Shall swell each breast with new-born joy;
Where blending differences shall meet
To clasp in union strong and sweet;
And soul greet soul, as face greets face,
While each, each other's good shall trace:
Yet, every varying gift must kiss,
To breathe the joy of mutual bliss.

Thence sprang the kind Creator's plan
To climax every boon to man,
And give to earth one heavenly ray
To gladden all his pilgrim way.

As one by one the stars came forth
And shone upon the new-made earth;
As softest zephyrs by were borne
Which ne'er had mingled with the storm,
And, laden with the rich perfume
Of Eden in her virgin bloom,
The first man sought sweet Nature's rest,
Alone, where all was good, unblest.

Then, we are told, from Adam's side
The Lord man's greatest want supplied.
No common clay the quick may trace
Of woman's loveliness and grace;
And near the heart God took the germ,
That soul to soul might ever yearn.

The young dawn over Eden broke,
And Adam from his slumber woke.
The morn's soft bloom his lids unsealed,
And God's best gift to man revealed.
And all for which his soul had sighed
Reposed in beauty by his side.

Then first had birth the sacred thrill
That rules the sons of Adam still.
On Eve's sweet lips, Love's kiss he pressed,
And called Heaven's latest work the best ;
For God to Eden's joys had given
A foretaste of the bliss of heaven.
And heaven's return will be to view
Their loving hearts forever true.

Where now the pall, the ache, the gloom,
Which rankled over Eden's bloom ?
Forever gone! and ties have birth
Throughout all time to hallow earth,—
Ties, that will fill the world with bliss
While Adam's sons Eve's daughters kiss.

    .   .   .   .   .   .

Woman! thy charms though frailties soil,
And imperfections round thee press,
Still, what were life without thy smile
To cheer, to comfort, and to bless!
Gloom would enfold man's mortal way,
And sadness every joy repel ;
Despair's black night would shroud Hope's day,—
Ay, even Eden would be hell !

1860.

AS WE GO MARCHING ON.

A Campaign Song.

WE'RE marching on to victory, as oft we've marched before :
The Democratic minions reel, and bite the dust once more,
And the Ku-Klux Southern devils feel the assassin's reign is o'er,
    As we go marching on.

        CHORUS.— Glory, glory hallelujah !
            Glory, glory hallelujah !
            Glory, glory hallelujah !
            Our cause is marching on.

Though Seymour's burning, butchering "*friends*," their hissing venom
    shed,
Though rebels howl whose hands to-day with loyal blood are red,
The Southern whip no more shall crack above the freeman's head,
    As we go marching on.

        CHORUS.

The blood-hounds of rebellion shall not hunt the loyal down,
For Fatherland and Liberty they faced war's lurid frown ;
Through tears and blood they bore the cross,—and peace their brows
    shall crown,
    As we go marching on.

        CHORUS.

We ask no boon but what we wish the whole broad land to bear,
But justice for the leal and true demands our grateful care ;
The loyal souls through freedom's night shall freedom's day-beams share
     As we go marching on.

     CHORUS.

By manhood's hopes and woman's prayers, by every Union grave,
O'er our broad land, our Union flag for equal rights shall wave :
The "corner-stone " on which we build will never be the slave,
     As we go marching on.

     CHORUS.

Wave on, thou flag of human hope, in freedom's sacred light,
No human bondage stains thy folds ; but, pledged to truth and right,
The Golden Rule shall gild each star, and temper every stripe,
     As we go marching on.

     CHORUS.

1868.

COMMEMORATION HYMN.

TUNE.—" A mighty fortress is our God."

I.

THE God of Nations is our stay,
   His hand has been our guiding ;
He leads us in his own good way,
   Our hearts in his confiding.
He was our shining light
In tribulation's night ;
When human hope grew dim,
Our trust was firm in him,
   And he vouchsafed the victory.

II.

The line and plummet of his rule
   Has rent Oppression's fetter :
Must tears forever be the school
   That God is God forever ?
His children he will keep,
His judgments never sleep ;
The ages are his own,
And Justice is his throne,
   The Lord is God forever !

III.

We saw him not,—we strove alone,
　　We sank, weak, worn, and gory;
We reared Emancipation's throne,—
　　HE CROWNED US WITH HIS GLORY!
His was the guiding hand,
He led the noble band
Who battled in his might
For Liberty and Right,
　　And Freedom made eternal!

IV.

Great God! be thou our bulwark still,
　　The tower of our salvation:
Still may our hearts discern thy will,
　　Still keep and bless our nation.
May Peace with Justice blend,
May Right her realm extend,
May Freedom find a shrine
Fast by the throne of Time,
　　And Heaven will guard our nation.

1871.

THE BURNING OF CHICAGO.

THE flames burst around as if hell had been rent,
  Hissing, leaping, and roaring like demons at play,
Mocking man like a fiend, e'en by granite unspent.
  The toils of an age lapping up in a day.

In vast smoking piles, her proud industry lies :
  The cottage, the mansion, the palace of trade,
The temples which pointed so late to the skies,
  In scorching and blistering ruins are laid.

Despatch wings despatch but our hearts to appall,
  And flash thy calamity over the land ;
But the angel in man leaps to life at thy call
  For help, and outreaches the brotherly hand.

Swift, swift o'er your courses, ye chariots of fire,
  Leap forth with the life-freighted burdens of love ;
For man, with his servants, the rail and the wire,
  In the dire hour of need may be almost a God !

Yet the flame-riven hearts by hot Michigan's shore
  Despair and misfortune to tatters will rend ;
Loving homes and proud marts once again to restore,
  Western manhood will pour out its wealth to the end.

Her future, unshadowed, will rise from the flames,
  A multiplied marvel of wonder and might ;
And again will her glory ascend from the plains,
  Lifted up as a crystallized dream of the night.

1871.

THE GATHERING CLOUD.

SCARCE bigger than a threatening hand
   Columbia marks the gathering cloud :
Shall its fell gloom o'erspread the land,
   Bid Progress halt, and Freedom shroud ?

Shall we subdue the morning light,
   And fetter education's ray ?
Shall moleish vision yield to night,
   The night that mantles Roman sway ?

Shall Superstition be the school
   To train and warp the mind of youth ?
Or independent Reason rule,
   And Knowledge lead the way to truth ?

The pillar of the nation's strength
   Is grounded in the Public School :
Will Romish craft prevail at length,
   That sacred fane shall priesthood rule ?

At Rome's dictation shall we kneel,
   And yield supine to Popish claims ?
Shall age-linked craft our birthright steal,
   And blast our hopes and forge our chains ?

Shades of the reverend Pilgrim dead,
  Who reared in prayer the Church and School,
Shall soaring Truth be cowled and led,
  Or Reason cringe where taught to rule?

Who rent the bonds of Church and State?
  Who reared, Intelligence, thy fanes?
What seed, Columbia, made thee great?
  Who bore the torch which Freedom flames?

Shall this inheritance be thrust,
  A sop, to priestly power and greed?
*Who bates one jot of this great trust
  On mildewed heritage would feed!*

The garnering ages are a shrine
  Where not alone the living kneel:
Down the unoutlined vault of Time,
  The Future wings her mute appeal.

As mighty sentinels of God,
  Earth's generations come and go;
And each with vengeance bares the rod
  That proves to human weal a foe.

Our Fathers planted: we enjoy,
  And broadly gather while they sleep;
And what they reared their sons will try
  To safely guard, and surely keep!

1872.

STANZAS.

Stern winter not always is sheeted in ice,
  And summer has more than showers ;
And poor is the heart that can never rejoice,
  Or that gathers the nettles for flowers.

Cheer up! with a brave, loving smile let us meet
  The duties of life as they glide ;
When with courage and beauty our lives are replete,
  God ever is close by our side.

                                          1872.

HURRAH FOR THE BEACH.

Hurrah for the beach! the glorious beach!
Where the briny waves to the greensward reach;
Where the marvellous waters ebb and flow,
And the sacred winds of the ocean blow
O'er the heaving main, full of tonic wealth,
And rich with the blessings of bounding health;
Where the foaming surges break and roll
As pure and as white as a maiden's soul.
Sweep gratefully up from your purified home,
O beautiful Sea! with your breakers and foam;
Sweep over the floor of the sanded shore,
Or high on the rocks of creation roar,
Which are lifted sublime by the Almighty hand,
Thy bosom to grace and ennoble thy strand:
Though ye angrily toss or peacefully sleep,
For me there is ever a smile on the deep.

1872.

SCATTER THE FLOWERS.

SCATTER the flowers,
Our Father's smiles,
   On the soldier's grave:
Sweet as his care,
Pure as his love,
   Is the sleep of the brave.

Their memories green
Our hearts will keep
   In immortal beauty:
Each hallowed grave
Is an angel's call
   To unfaltering duty.

The lives they lived,
The deaths they died,
   Will remembered be,
While the grasses grow,
And the rivers flow
   To the great, wide sea.

No more may Wrong
His sceptre wield,
   Nor ever Justice sleep:
Their sacred trusts
Our souls will guard,
   And Freedom's portal keep.

1875.

THE SABBATH BELLS.

I.

How SWEETLY on the morning air
To worship call the Sabbath bells ;
And tender as an angel's prayer
O'er hill and vale their music swells.

II.

The flowers which from the ground arise,
The living robes which earth adorn,
The sacred blue that paints the skies,
Seem holier on the Sabbath morn.

III.

Send over hill and vale, sweet bells,
Your call to worship and to prayer :
Heaven's benison benignly dwells
With every listening pilgrim there.

1875.

LINES WRITTEN IN DIFFICULTY.

Be calm and strong, my soul :
When keen anxieties beset thy way,
And difficulty looms, height upon height,
Like giant mountains upon mountains piled,
Let not the gathering shadows of despair
Thy vision dim, or hide thy Father's smiles.
When trial like an avalanche descends,
Call on thy noblest manhood to stand forth
And hurl it back, or by the shock be crushed.
Whatever may befall, let nothing shake
Thy steadfast faith in God's protecting care :
But bravely hope, and bravely do thy best,
Then, with an angel's trust, wait for the light :
For ever would my soul on Thee repose,
And nestle with a credence naught can shake
In thy unslumbering, gracious providence.
When racked and worn, dejected, crushed, soul-sick,
When human strength can bear and do no more,
And panting, struggling effort finds itself
Dashed headlong on the iron rail of life,
Bewildered, blinded, stunned,— then let me stop,
Stop short ! and take anew the bearings of
This little span.

Does judgment not cry, Hold!
When health, like chaff, is blown to every wind,
And constitutions seem but worthless grist
To feed the hopper of life's grinding mill?
Weigh well this blind, mad, withering haste,
This cold, unpitying, swirling greed of gain!
Weigh even the stern duty that impels
To spread the board of plenty in our homes.
Nature but little needs, and well can spare
The rack and toil of artificial wants.
The pampered appetite is never full,
And craving luxury is never cloyed:
The more we nurse vagaries of desire
The faster will dissatisfaction breed.

What boots it all, this wild, relentless rush,—
Relentless as Niagara's plunge and roar?
Though competition, merciless, strides on;
Though effort every sinew overstrain,
Yet still perplexity bars every road;
Though obloquy and malice hedge our way;
Though thorny sickness pales the inward fire;
Though, last of all, where sorrow's bottom stops,
Where naught can underlie or get behind
To mar the passionless repose of death,—
Then let the heart of manhood beat, not swift
And wild, but calm and strong; and, howsoever dark
The way, keep in the soul — clear, firm, serene —
The grand, triumphant faith that mountains moves,
The trust that led the Pilgrim Fathers o'er
The surging seas, and bade their spirits sing

Above the storm ! So to the bruised heart
Shall rest and light and sacred healing come.
So light and rest and peace and joy we find ;
The crooked paths of Providence grow straight ;
The cup of disappointment has no dregs ;
The sting is drawn from unrequited aims ;
And gall and bitterness find no lodgement
In the heart that keeps a childlike, trusting
Faith in God's directing and protecting care.

1875.

LINES WRITTEN IN AN ALBUM.

DEAR GERTIE, I must not reveal all the love
  The heart of a father may bear ;
Some would deem me but weak, though my darling would know
  Every wish of my heart is a prayer.

So loving and thoughtful, so tender and wise,
  Like a dear little woman you seem :
To be frank, you appear in your fond father's eyes
  As if Nature had made you a queen.

Noble aims on your brow as a coronet wear,
  And the sweet name of woman adorn :
Be as true as the blush on the rose, and as fair
  As the dew on the lily of morn.

You throw me back blessings and crown me with mirth
  By striving to be all you seem :
In wisdom, simplicity, sweetness, and worth
  Be ever and always a queen.

CANTON, March 23, 1879.

SUGGESTED BY THE UNVEILING OF THE LINCOLN EMANCIPATION STATUE IN BOSTON.

UNVEIL the proud emblem of Freedom,
Let the sweet light of God round it play :
The chain of the bondsman is broken,
O'er the night of the slave rolls the day.
No Juggernaut tyranny drives o'er the weak ;
Nevermore may a blush mantle Liberty's cheek.

Immortality guardeth her children,
Blessings hallow the places they trod,—
With a tear for the Heaven-guided Lincoln,
Humanity bows and thanks God.
Benign as the blessings of all-healing grace,
His grand benediction is lifting a race.

This shrine is most fittingly lifted
Where first beamed the star of the slave,
For here the great-souled and the gifted
The death-blow to tyranny gave.
Here, reviled, jeered, and hated, they fearlessly trod,
Sustained and consoled by their conscience and God.

Here the great sun of Garrison rose,
Here the lightnings of Phillips were hurled,
Sumner went forth for Liberty's throes,
And her battle-flags Andrew unfurled.
Wills of adamant here were for Freedom arrayed,
And here the dark tide of the nation was stayed.

They were rooted and fixed as the mountains
For Liberty, Justice, and Right ;
Their clarions rang through the nation,
The demon of bondage to smite.
And in vain sought the nation the Union to save
Till the shackles were struck from the limbs of the slave.

1879.

THE BATTLE OF LIFE.

Human life is a battle, and sometimes the strife
   No truce to the struggle, no lull will impart ;
And misgivings worm into the sedges of life,
   And sadness gets hold of the strings of the heart.

There are things that we would, that no striving can do,
   There are hopes and fond aims that we cannot attain ;
From our dreams we awake, then our dreamings renew :
   So life ever goes on with its pleasure and pain.

Our resolves roll and break like the wild-beating surge ;
   They are dashed on the shore, and then backward they roll :
So the tides of our lives their resistless floods urge,
   But again they will ebb beyond human control.

Yet the spirit of man has a realm of delight,
   Where it wills and it rules, and exults in its joy :
'Tis the realm of the heart, it is love's sacred light,
   Which blesses the earth and makes radiant the sky.

For the spirit with courage and vigor will burn,
   When we think of the loved ones that hallow our way ;
And the heart, true and strong, to surrender would spurn,
   When the burdens grow light as the children's at play.

To soften the pillow where nightly they sleep,
  To carpet with blessings their pathway in life,
May this be the heritage long we may keep,
  Then welcome the battle and sweet be the strife.

No repining, no whining, no fretting complaint,
  The head must be clear, the hand willing and strong ;
For omnipotent will overrides all restraint,
  So the night may grow short, and the day may be long.

1881.

THE LOVED ONES AT HOME.

WHEREVER my footsteps may wander,
Wherever in life I may roam,
The delight and the joy of my soul is to think
Of my beautiful loved ones at home.

If the battle of life clouds my vision
When the burden o'er-heavy has grown,
It fills me with courage and cheers me anew
When I think of the loved ones at home.

When the light of my life is departing
To the realms of the mighty unknown,
I know that my spirit will linger to bless
My sorrowful loved ones at home.

And in the great world over yonder,
Wheresoever permitted to roam,
Every uplifted prayer to the Father I'll bear
From my suppliant loved ones at home.

When in danger and darkness and trial,
Think not ye are ever alone ;
For, if spirit through silence to spirit may come,
Light will beam on my loved ones at home.

I shall meet the long lost and the loving,
Where partings no more will be known ;
And close to the living, when called, I will stand,
To welcome the angels from home.

1882.

ANCHORINGS.

HEARTS sound at the core to true honor will cleave
　Through life's Sisyphus toilings, through conflict and wrong ;
Though detraction may cloud, and though praise may deceive,
　Yet the smile of the soul is the strength of the strong.

Evil always is evil,—good reigns as the sun ;
　Truth is never a lie,—right is always the same ;
God's lines never cross, through the ages they run,
　And girdle them round as with cordons of flame.

Hate barbs her own breast and grinds day into night,
　While love — life's best angel — pure blessedness sheds ;
Philanthropy's hill-tops are flooded with light,
　And self-sacrifice hallows the ground that it treads.

Amidst life's mutations, its triumphs and tears,
　Marriage bells and despair, bliss and woe side by side,
With want, pain, and heartaches surcharging the years,—
　What a bauble is pomp ! for but scorn is poor pride !

Sick and tired is the heart of the jargon of creeds,
　Of sectarian bitterness, wrangling, and strife ;
But it welcomes the thought that will meet human needs,
　That will character build and ennoble the life.

O'er the rivalries fierce, and the rush of the mart,
    May thought, genius born, solace, cheer and expand ;
And may nature's fond charms softly steal through the heart,
    While perfection and beauty encircle the land.

I wist not, nor care, what the multitude say,
    But the noble in action and thought I revere :
Proud Duty points out her invincible way,
    And her paths by the fixed stars of God are made clear.

While all nature's voices with gladness may thrill,
    While my soul with the flowers a sweet kinship can claim,
While the loved ones I live for their radiance instil,
    But a rattle is praise, and no venom has blame.

The soul holds communings where eye cannot see,
    And her sacred revealings to silence belong ;
But this message she often has whispered to me :
    In endeavor be faithful, in trial be strong.

But we walk not alone, angels lovingly guide,
    Though no presence we trace, and no voices we hear ;
When life's passions are hushed, they are close by our side,—
    Though unheard and unseen, yet we know they are near.

1883.